Punk Wig

Lori Ries

Illustrated by Erin Eitter Kono

BOYDS MILLS PRESS
Honesdale, Pennsylvania

The author and illustrator wish to thank Pamela Schmid, RN,
for reviewing the text and illustrations.

Boyds Mills Press, Inc.
815 Church Street
Honesdale, Pennsylvania 18431
Printed in China

Library of Congress Cataloging-in-Publication Data

Ries, Lori Anne.
  Punk wig / Lori Ries ; illustrated by Erin Eitter Kono. — 1st ed.
    p. cm.
ISBN 978-1-59078-486-0 (hardcover : alk. paper)
1. Cancer—Juvenile literature. 2. Children of cancer patients—Juvenile literature.
I. Kono, Erin Eitter, ill. II. Title.

RC264.R54 2008
618.92'994—dc22
                              2007017688

First edition
The text of this book is set in 15-point Sabon.
The illustrations are done in watercolors.

10 9 8 7 6 5 4 3 2 1

With love to Cate, Carson, Dan, and Danielle, who truly have
something to celebrate, and special thanks to my family and
all who helped with this book
                                                    —L.R.

For Caitlyn, Kirk, Nina, and everyone
who inspires laughter in adversity
                                    —E.E.K.

My mom's got alien blobs inside her. They're called cancer.
She's going to the hospital to get the alien blobs zapped with medicine.

Mom has lots of flowers in her room. The roses are from Dad, the daisies are from Grandma, and there is a big sunflower picked by me. Her table is filled with cards, and a heart-shaped balloon floats over her bed.

I can see the park outside her window. "There are ducks swimming in the pond, and people are feeding them bread," I say. "Yes, I know. The view is lovely," Mom says.

When I push the buttons on Mom's bed, her head goes up and down, up and down. I make her feet come up, too! "This is cool! Can I have a bed like this one?"

Mom shows me the tube for the zapping medicine. Then she tells me something funny. "This medicine will make my hair fall out," she says.

"You mean you're going to be bald?"

"For a while, until my hair grows back. I will wear a wig."

When Mom comes home, she is very tired, but every day she feels a little better. Sometimes I play checkers with her.

I bring her lunch on a tray and give her the gorilla cup that was mine when I was little.

"I hope you like peanut butter and jelly," I say.

"My favorite," Mom whispers.

One morning, I wake up to something funny. Mom has a feather duster on her head. She is feeling very good today and just a little bit silly.

"Let's get hairy," she says. "Today is wig day." Mom grabs her sun hat. "I hope I remember how to drive the car," she says.

"You've forgotten?"

"Well, if I have, you can drive for me."

Harriett's Hair is the hairiest place I've ever seen! There is big hair, short hair, hair with spikes, hair with curls—even itty-bitty top-of-the-head hair.

"This must be the hairiest place on earth," I say.

Mom looks at a large thick-haired wig. "They've probably got wigs for lions and wild buffalo," she says.

"And dinosaurs?"

"Dinosaurs are bald."

A lady comes from the back of the shop. "Welcome. I'm Harriett," she says. "Now, which one of you needs hair?"

Mom tries on a short straight wig.
I try on a brown curly one.
   "You look like a film star," Mom says.
   "You don't. You look like my mom."
   "Hmmm . . . I do, don't I?"
   She puts the wig back and looks at a row of party hair.

I laugh and laugh. "Now you look like a blue cotton-candy head!"

Mom laughs. "And you look like Elvis as a Martian," she says.

"Who's Elvis?" I ask.

Mom chases me with her hands out like
claws. "I'll get you, my pretty!" she shrieks,
wearing a long stringy wig.

"No, I'll get you! I'll send you into my dungeon!"
I walk stiff and moan like a monster.

"Let's get serious," says Mom. "How about this one?"
It's a long orange wig, spiky on the top.
"Yeah, I like it."
"I like it, too," Harriett says.

"My Punk Wig,
that's what we'll call it," Mom says.

We take Punk Wig home. Mom can't wait to show Dad.

Mom makes more trips to the hospital for alien-blob-zapping medicine. Sometimes she feels sick. That means the medicine is working.

At home Mom sometimes sits in the swing and
I push her. We like to talk.

When we go to the store, everyone stares at Punk Wig.
Mom smiles. She looks great in blue jeans and a black leather jacket.
"New do?" the checker asks. "I like it," she says.

I help carry out the groceries.
Punk Wig is as orange as our pumpkin.

Winter comes and the yard fills with snow.
I help Mom make a snowman.
  "He needs a hat," I say.
  "Not a hat. Let's give him hair."
  Punk Wig makes our snowman look fiery hot.

Mom tries to knock the hair off with snowballs.
"You'll ruin the wig," I say.
"No worries," Mom says. "My hair is growing."

It is spring. I am going with Mom to the doctor to get the results of her tests. She comes out with a big smile. All the alien blobs have gone away, and her hair is growing back!

Dad makes a happy-zappy surprise dinner.
"I've got something for you," Mom says to me.
She gives me a box.

WOO-HOO!
Punk Wig is MINE!